KU-350-901

Disney

WINNIE the POOH'S

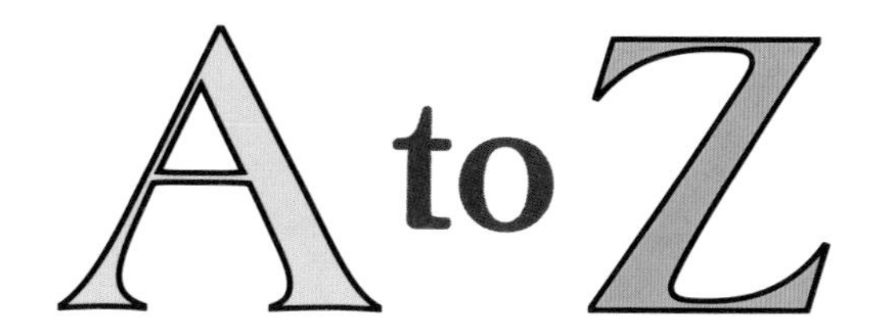

Ladybird books are widely available, but in case of difficulty may be ordered by post or telephone from:

Ladybird Books – Cash Sales Department
Littlegate Road Paignton Devon TQ3 3BE
Telephone 0803 554761

A catalogue record for this book is available from the British Library

First edition

Published by Ladybird Books Ltd Loughborough Leicestershire UK

Printed in EC

Disney

WINNIE the POOH'S

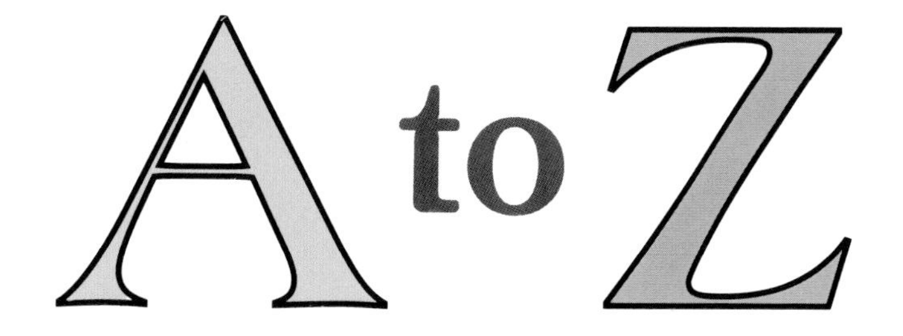

Ladybird

A

IS FOR ACORN

From atop an oak tree
In the Hundred Acre Wood
A little acorn fell
Right where Pooh Bear stood.

B

IS FOR BEAR

Some bears growl, some bears snort,
But Pooh Bear is the humming sort.

C

IS FOR CARROT

Carrots are so good to munch,
Rabbit grows them by the bunch.

D
IS FOR DOOR
In spring, Pooh's door is open wide
To let the sunshine come inside.

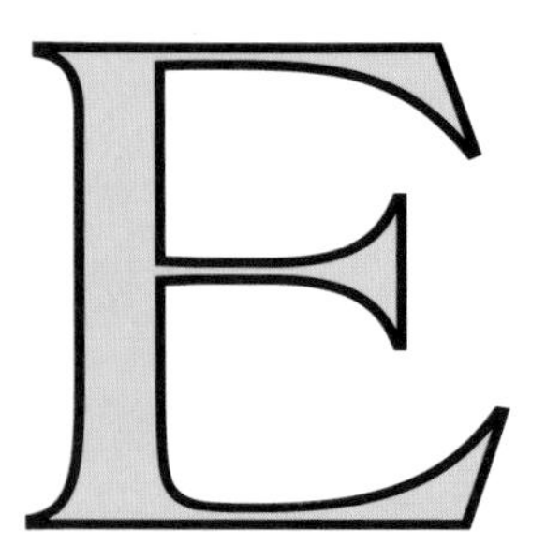

IS FOR EEYORE

Eeyore's looking gloomy,
Though why it's hard to say.
His friends have gathered round
To wish him *Happy Birthday!*

HAPPY BIRTHDAY
Eeyore

F

IS FOR FOOTPRINT

Our footprints always follow us
On days when it's been snowing.
They always show us where we've been,
But never where we're going.

G

IS FOR GOPHER

"Hello!" says Gopher to Winnie the Pooh.
"I've just come up to visit you!"

H IS FOR HONEY

"My favourite snack," says Winnie the Pooh,
"Is a jar of honey... or possibly two!"

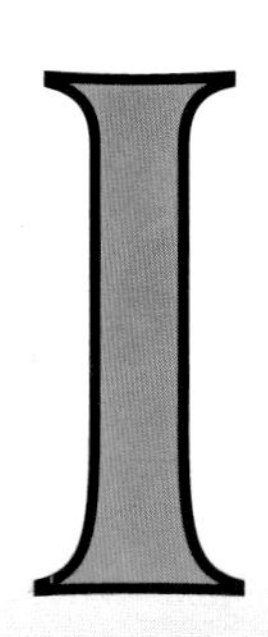

IS FOR ICE SKATE

Though others give him funny glances,
On ice skates Pooh Bear takes no chances.

J

IS FOR JUMP

Rum-tee-tiddle-tum, tiddle-tum-too,
When Kanga jumps, so does Roo!

K
IS FOR KITE
When the blustery autumn breezes blow,
Up in the air kites and Piglets go!

L IS FOR LADDER

A ladder is helpful
To go up and down trees,
When hunting for honey
Or running from bees.

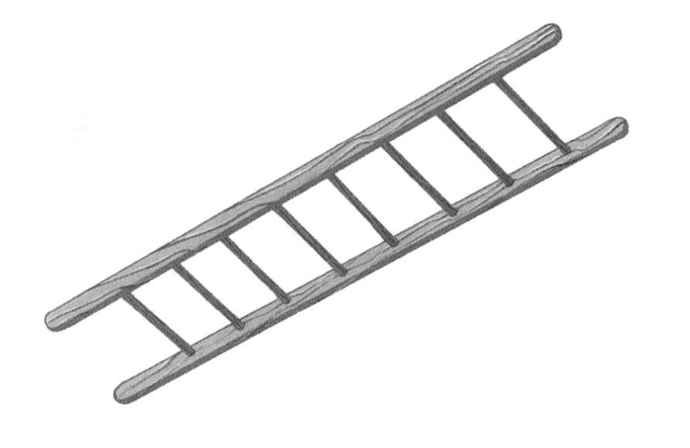

M

IS FOR MIRROR

"The bear in the mirror's
Quite clever," says Pooh,
"He knows how to copy
Whatever I do!"

N

IS FOR NOSE

Why have we,
Do you suppose,
Two eyes, two ears,
But just one nose?

O

IS FOR OWL

Owl likes to talk a lot –
He's really quite a bore!
He tells Pooh everything he knows –
And sometimes even more!

P

IS FOR PIGLET

Piglet is so very small,
Sometimes he can't be seen at all!

Q

IS FOR QUILT

Let it snow!
Let it storm!
Under his quilt
Pooh is cosy and warm!

R

IS FOR RABBIT

Rabbit is so very busy,
Watching him makes Pooh Bear dizzy!

S

IS FOR SEESAW

Never make a seesaw date
With a bear who's overweight!

T IS FOR TIGGER

Though winter's here
And birds don't sing,
Tigger's tail still
Has its spring!

IS FOR UMBRELLA

Clever Pooh is now afloat
In his own umbrella boat!

V
IS FOR VELVET
Piglet's velvet waistcoat
Is colourful and bright,
He wears it every Sunday –
And takes it off at night!

W

IS FOR WOOZLE

There's nothing to fear
From a Woozle, it seems,
They're only found
In Pooh Bear's dreams!

X
IS FOR XYLOPHONE
Pooh's made a honeypot xylophone,
And, oh, it has the sweetest tone.

Y

IS FOR YAWN

Put on your nightcap, sleepyhead!
You're yawning, so it's time for bed.

Z

IS

FOR

ZZZZ!

A sound that Pooh
makes in his bed,
Begins and ends
with the letter Z.